Famous Myths and Legends of the World

Myths and Legends of

ANCIENT EGYPT

WORLD
BOOK

a Scott Fetzer company
Chicago
www.worldbook.com

World Book, Inc.
180 North LaSalle Street
Suite 900
Chicago, Illinois 60601
USA

For information about other World Book publications, visit our website at **www.worldbook.com** or call **1-800-967-5325.**

Library of Congress Cataloging-in-Publication Data

Myths and legends of ancient Egypt.
    pages cm. -- (Famous myths and legends of the world)
    Summary: "Myths and legends from ancient Egypt. Features include information about the history and culture behind the myths, pronunciations, lists of deities, word glossary, further information, and index"-- Provided by publisher.
    Includes index.
    ISBN 978-0-7166-2633-6
    1. Mythology, Egyptian--Juvenile literature. 2. Legends--Egypt--Juvenile literature. I. World Book, Inc. II. Series: Famous myths and legends of the world.
    BL2441.3.M98 2015
    299'.3113--dc23
                                2015014763

Set ISBN: 978-0-7166-2625-1
E-book ISBN: 978-0-7166-2645-9 (EPUB3)

Printed in China by PrintWORKS Global Services, Shenzhen, Guangdong
2nd printing May 2016

Writer: Scott A. Leonard

Staff for World Book, Inc.
Executive Committee
President: Jim O'Rourke
Vice President and Editor in Chief: Paul A. Kobasa
Vice President, Finance: Donald D. Keller
Vice President, Marketing: Jean Lin
Director, International Sales: Kristin Norell
Director, Licensing Sales: Edward Field
Director, Human Resources: Bev Ecker

Editorial
Manager, Annuals/Series Nonfiction: Christine Sullivan
Managing Editor, Annuals/Series Nonfiction:
    Barbara Mayes
Administrative Assistant: Ethel Matthews
Manager, Indexing Services: David Pofelski
Manager, Contracts & Compliance
    (Rights & Permissions): Loranne K. Shields

Manufacturing/Production
Manufacturing Manager: Sandra Johnson
Production/Technology Manager: Anne Fritzinger
Proofreader: Nathalie Strassheim

Graphics and Design
Senior Art Director: Tom Evans
Coordinator, Design Development and Production:
    Brenda Tropinski
Senior Designers: Matthew Carrington,
    Isaiah W. Sheppard, Jr.
Media Researcher: Jeff Heimsath
Manager, Cartographic Services: Wayne K. Pichler
Senior Cartographer: John M. Rejba

Staff for Brown Bear Books Ltd
Managing Editor: Tim Cooke
Editorial Director: Lindsey Lowe
Children's Publisher: Anne O'Daly
Design Manager: Keith Davis
Designer: Mike Davis
Picture Manager: Sophie Mortimer

CONTENTS

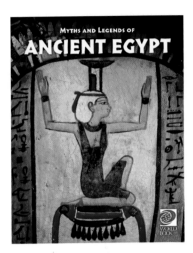

An image of the goddess Isis decorates the case of the mummy of an ancient Egyptian priest. Ancient Egyptians worshiped Isis as the protector of the dead and as the divine mother.

De Agostini Picture Library/ G. Dagli Orti/Bridgeman Images

Note to Readers:

Phonetic pronunciations have been inserted into the myths and legends in this volume to make reading the stories easier and to give the reader some of the flavor of the ancient Egyptian culture the stories represent. See page 64 for a pronunciation key.

The myths and legends retold in this volume are written in a creative way to provide an engaging reading experience and approximate the artistry of the originals. Many of these stories were not written down but were recited by storytellers from generation to generation. Even when some of the stories came to be written down they likely did not feature phonetic pronunciations for challenging names and words! We hope the inclusion of this material will improve rather than distract from your experience of the stories.

Some of the figures mentioned in the myths and legends in this volume are described on page 60 in the section "Deities of Ancient Egypt." In addition, some unusual words in the text are defined in the Glossary on page 62.

INTRODUCTION

Since the earliest times, people have told stories to try to explain the world in which they lived. These stories are known as myths. Myths try to answer such questions as, How was the world created? Who were the first people? Where did animals come from? Why does the sun rise and set? Why is the land devastated by storms or drought? Today, people often rely on science to answer many of these questions. But in earlier times—and in some parts of the world today—people have explained natural events using stories about gods, goddesses, nature spirits, and heroes.

The World of the Ancient Egyptians, page 10

Myths are different from folk tales and legends. Folk tales are fictional stories about animals or human beings. Most of these tales are not set in any particular time or place, and they begin and end in a certain way. For example, many English folk tales begin with the phrase "Once upon a time" and end with "They lived happily ever after." Legends are set in the real world, in the present or the historical past. Legends distort the truth, but they are based on real people or events.

Myths, in contrast, typically tell of events that have taken place in the remote past. Unlike legends, myths have also played—and often continue to play—an important role in a society's religious life. Although legends may have religious themes, most are not religious in nature. The people of a society may tell folk tales and

4

legends for amusement, without believing them. But they usually consider their myths sacred and completely true.

Most myths concern *divinities* or *deities* (divine beings). These divinities have powers far greater than those of any human being. At the same time, however, many gods, goddesses, and heroes of mythology have human characteristics. They are guided by such emotions as love and jealousy, and they may experience birth and death. Mythological figures may even look like human beings. Often, the human qualities of the divinities reflect a society's ideals. Good gods and goddesses have the qualities a society admires, and evil ones have the qualities it dislikes. In myths, the actions of these divinities influence the world of humans for better or for worse.

Myths may seem very strange. They sometimes seem to take place in a world that is both like our world and unlike it. Time can go backward and forward, so it is sometimes difficult to tell in what order events happen. People may be dead and alive at the same time.

Myths were originally passed down from generation to generation by word of mouth. Partly for this reason, there are often different versions of the same story. Many myths across cultures share similar themes, such as a battle between good and evil. But the myths of a society generally reflect the landscape, climate, and society in which the storytellers lived.

The World of Isis, page 16

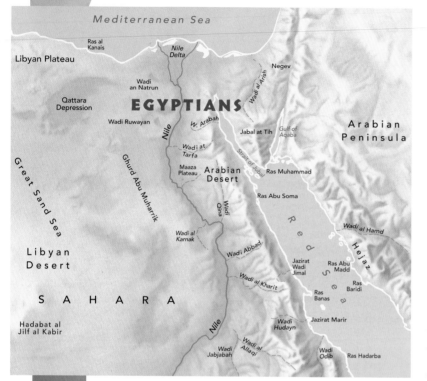

Myths tell people about their distant history. They show people how to behave and find their way. As teaching tools, myths help to prepare children for adulthood.

Myths of Ancient Egypt

The Nile River was an important source of Egyptian mythology as well as water. As the Nile flows northward through Egypt, it creates a narrow ribbon of fertile land in the midst of a great desert. The sharp contrast between the fertility along the river and the wasteland of the desert became a basic theme of Egyptian mythology.

The ancient Egyptian civilization developed in the Nile River Valley and in the Nile River Delta. It depended on the yearly flood of the river to keep the land fertile enough to grow crops. To the east and the west of the river lie generally inhospitable deserts.

The Egyptians had many gods. Some were worshiped in a particular town, but others were important throughout the whole country. Over the long history of ancient Egypt, myths changed as the importance of various gods rose or fell. The myths generally concern the creation of the world and the development of their most important deities, Re, Osiris, Isis, Horus, and the evil god Seth. Many animals appear in Egyptian mythology. The falcon and the scarab, or dung beetle, were two animals that symbolized the Sun God. The Egyptians considered the cat and the crocodile to be divine.

There are also stories about the fate of the dead. The Egyptians developed one of the first religions to emphasize life after death. In fact, they believed that they could enjoy life after death. This belief sometimes led to much preparation for death and burial. It resulted, for example, in the construction of the pyramids and other great tombs for kings and queens. The Egyptians also believed that the bodies of the dead had to be preserved for the next life, and so they *mummified* (embalmed and dried) corpses to prevent them from decaying. They filled their tombs with clothing and other items for use in the afterlife.

The divinities of ancient Egypt and the myths about them may have had a long-lasting effect. During the 1300's B.C., the pharaoh Amenhotep IV chose a little-known god named Aten as the only god of Egypt. The Egyptians stopped worshiping Aten after the pharaoh died. But some scholars believe the worship of this one divinity lingered among the people of Israel, who had settled in Egypt. These scholars have suggested that the cult of Aten may have inspired the Jewish, Christian, and Islamic belief in one God.

The World of the
Scribe, page 58

Although many of the stories in this book appear simple at first glance, they are layered with meaning. Each retelling of the story reveals a new meaning. Understanding these myths is necessary for any kind of understanding of the societies that created them. By studying myths, we can learn how different societies have answered basic questions about the world and the individual's place in it.

THE CREATION OF
THE GODS AND THE WORLD

The Egyptians believed that many gods controlled Earth and the Heavens, but it was the god Atum who created life.

In the beginning, there was Nu (noo), dark water without end. From within the emptiness that was Nu, the Shining One arose. At dawn, he is Khephera (keh puhr uh), the One Who Begins. At noon, he is Re (ray), the All-Seeing Eye. At sunset, he is Atum (AH tuhm), the One Who Completes.

Atum arose first in the darkness, glowing warm in the emptiness of Nu. His arising created the benben stone, the hill upon which Earth is founded. In a mighty explosion, Atum sneezed out Shu (shoo), God of Wind, and his lovely consort, Tefnut (TEHF not), Giver of Rain.

Atum spoke, and Earth and the Heavens appeared as Geb (gehb), the Earth Father, and Nut (noot), the Sky Mother.

They embraced for long ages, giving birth to the gods Isis (Y sihs), Osiris (oh SY rihs), and Seth (sehth). In time, airy Shu lifted Nut, the Sky Mother, into the vault of heaven. Nut's toes now rest upon the eastern horizon; her fingertips touch the west. At night, the stars shine in Nut's body. Below, green Geb gazes lovingly up at blue Nut.

Before Geb and Nut emerged, Shu and Tefnut drifted away from their father, Atum, upon the waves of Nu. Atum, who has only one eye, plucked it out and sent it upon the waves in search of his children. When at last Atum's All-Seeing Eye found them, it guided them back to their father. Atum felt such joy when they returned that his eye wept tears. These salty drops struck the benben stone and became human beings.

Others say that life came about in a less accidental way. They say that whatever Atum spoke became real, whether on land or in the sea or in the heavens. That which crawls, walks, swims, or flies sprang forth at the sound of his holy word. But all agree, that people sprang from the tears of his All-Seeing Eye.

9

The World of THE ANCIENT EGYPTIANS

Ancient Egypt was the birthplace of one of the world's first civilizations, with the first Egyptian cities appearing by around 3150 B.C. Ancient Egypt thrived for over 2,000 years and so became one of the longest lasting civilizations in history. The civilization reached its height around 1300 B.C.

LIFE-GIVING RIVER

Ancient Egypt owed its existence to the Nile River. Egypt's civilization developed, in large part, because of the river's regular annual floods. The floodwaters carried rich soil into the fields along the river. The ancient Egyptians called their country *Kemet* (keh MEHT) meaning *Black Land*, after the dark soil. Because the Nile's floods were predictable, farmers were able to plant and harvest enough crops to support a large population.

Boats and barges on the Nile River were the chief means of transportation for the ancient Egyptians. The earliest Egyptian boats were made of papyrus reeds (above). Moved first by poles, they later were powered by rowers with oars. By about 3200 B.C., the Egyptians had invented sails. About 3000 B.C., they started to build ships with wooden planks. Traditional wooden boats called feluccas (fuh LUHK uhs) (left), narrow ships with triangular sails, navigated the Nile in ancient times, as they do today.

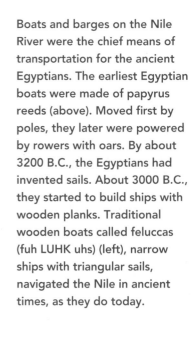

KINGS AND PHARAOHS

People today often refer to a king of ancient Egypt as a *pharaoh*. But the ancient Egyptians themselves did not begin to call their king a pharaoh until sometime between 1554 and 1304 B.C., some 1,500 years after the beginning of their civilization. The ancient Egyptians believed that each king was the falcon-headed god Horus (HAWR uhs) in human form. This belief helped strengthen the authority of the kings.

A huge statue of Ramses (RAM seez) II is one of eight statues of this celebrated king that guard the entrances to the two Temples of Abu Simbel (AH boo SIHM buhl) in southern Egypt. Ramses, who reigned from about 1279 to 1213 B.C., built the temples for his worship as a god.

Three of the largest and best preserved ancient Egyptian pyramids (left) stand at Giza (GEE zuh) on the west bank of the Nile River outside Cairo. From about 2700 to 1700 B.C., the bodies of Egyptian kings were buried inside or beneath one of these structures in a secret chamber that was filled with treasures of gold and precious objects.

Isis Learns
RE'S SECRET

Isis was one of the Egyptians' most important goddesses. She used witchcraft to gain power over the other gods.

When all was yet a watery chaos, Nu (noo) gave shining Re (ray), the Sun God, a secret name. It was from this name that Re's divine power flowed. After Re created the other gods and settled Earth with living things, he reigned on Earth.

Like Re, her grandfather, the goddess Isis (Y sihs) dwelled on Earth, but she appeared in a woman's body. After a time, Isis grew weary of her flesh and desired instead to dwell among the gods in eternity. But even though she was already a powerful witch, Isis needed Re's secret name to join the gods.

Re's long life had drained his vitality. His human form had grown feeble. His head and hands trembled. He drooled. And yet he lived on.

One day, while following Re, Isis gathered some of the saliva that dribbled from his mouth to the ground. She combined it with the dust on which it lay, molded the mud into the shape of a spear, and baked it. Through some magic that Isis worked, the spear became a poisonous snake, and Isis placed it on the ground where she knew Re was sure to walk.

Soon afterward, the snake bit Re. Venom entered Re's body, and he roared with pain. His body shook, and his teeth chattered. After he had mastered his pain, he gathered the other gods.

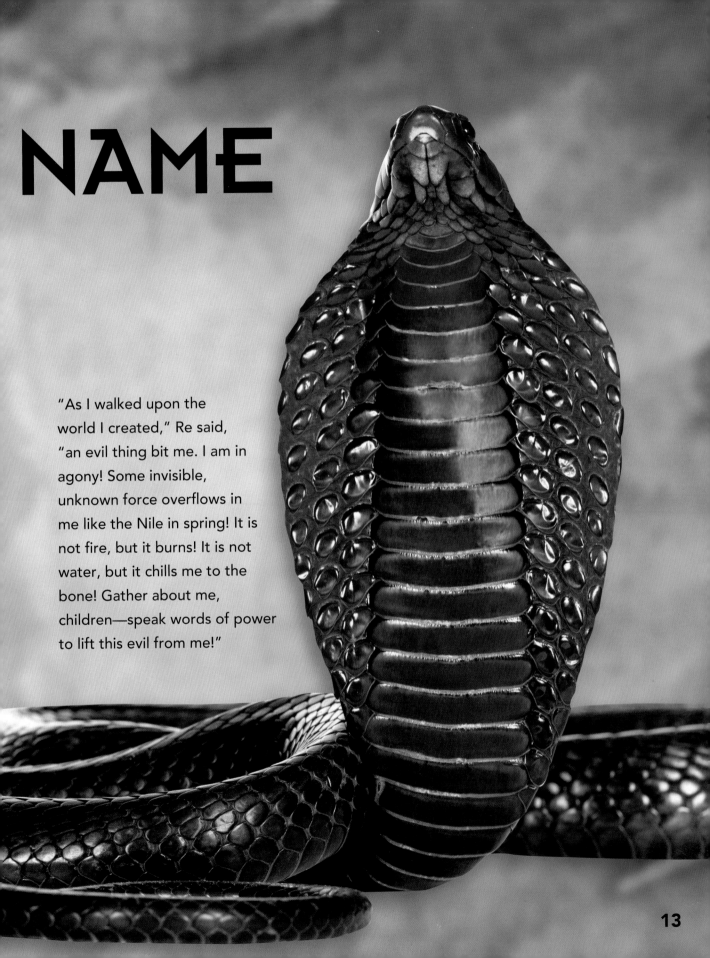

NAME

"As I walked upon the world I created," Re said, "an evil thing bit me. I am in agony! Some invisible, unknown force overflows in me like the Nile in spring! It is not fire, but it burns! It is not water, but it chills me to the bone! Gather about me, children—speak words of power to lift this evil from me!"

14

The gods gathered, filled with sorrow. Only Isis was unmoved by Re's pain. "Holy father," Isis said, "a serpent—one of the creatures you created—has bitten you. I will weave spells to defeat your enemy. I will overpower the snake's venom with the brightness of your glory."

Isis spoke mighty words to ease Re's pain, words that ordinarily had the power to resurrect the dead. But Re continued to writhe in pain, sweat dripping from his brow.

"Holy father," Isis said, "My power is not strong enough to defeat this enemy. You must reveal to me your secret name. If I have your powerful name, I can relieve your pain!"

Re told her some of his many names, hoping for relief. "I am the Great Father of the Shining Immortal Ones," he cried. "I created every living thing on land, in the air, and beneath the waves. When I open my eyes, there is light. When I close them, there is darkness. I am Khephera (keh puhr uh) the Scarab (SKAR uhb) at dawn! I am Re at high noon! I am Atum (AH tuhm) by sunset!"

The magical power of Re's words was overwhelming. But he did not reveal his secret name, so the poison continued its work. Although he was on the point of death, Isis felt no sorrow. Her desire for power was greater than any sadness for Re's pain. "Divine father," she said, "you have not revealed your secret name. Without it, I lack the strength to heal you."

At last Re could endure no more. "By my will, Isis shall be given my secret name. It shall leave my heart and enter hers."

As soon as Re said this, he vanished from sight. Mandjet (mand jeht), the Boat of Millions of Years, in which Re travels across the sky, was suddenly empty, and Earth was plunged into a profound darkness. When Re's secret name passed into her heart, Isis spoke: "Depart, O venom, from Re! Flow out of his flesh and be spilled on the ground!" And Re was restored to his youth, and his heart was freed from sorrow.

The World of ISIS

Magic was central to ancient Egyptian religion, and Isis (Y sihs) had the most powerful magic of all the gods. For most Egyptians, Isis was the most important god. They called her the "Great Mother" and the "Queen of Heaven." Isis was seen as the ideal wife and mother, as well as the goddess of nature and magic. She was often shown as a woman wearing a headdress of cow horns with the disk of the sun between them. After the Egyptian civilization declined, Isis's cult spread throughout the ancient Roman world.

The Temple to Isis at Philae (FY lee) (right) was built in the 200's B.C. The temple was threatened with destruction by the construction of the Aswan (AS wahn) High Dam in the 1960's, which flooded the island (Philae) on which it sat. The temple was disassembled block by block and moved safely to the island of Agilka.

FEMALE RULERS

The position of king in ancient Egypt was inherited. It passed to the eldest son of the king's chief wife. Many Egyptian kings had several other wives, called *lesser wives*, at the same time. Some chief wives gave birth to daughters but no sons, and several of those daughters claimed the right to the throne. At least four women became the ruler of ancient Egypt.

The goddess Isis (in white, far left) accompanies Queen Nefertiti (NEHF uhr TEE tee), wife of Pharaoh Akhenaten (AH kuh NAH tehn), in a painting from the 1300's B.C.

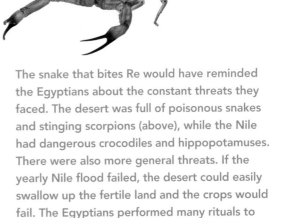

SCARAB BEETLES

Scarabs (SKAR uhbz) are beetles. Some kinds of scarab breed in *dung* (manure). They roll this dung into pellets, in which they lay their eggs. The *larvae* (immature forms) use the dung as food. The Egyptians saw the pellet of the scarab as a symbol of the world. They saw the beetles' horns as emblems of the rays of the sun. The sacred scarab also symbolized resurrection and immortality. The Egyptians carved figures of the insects from stone or metal and used them as charms. Such figures were also called scarabs.

The snake that bites Re would have reminded the Egyptians about the constant threats they faced. The desert was full of poisonous snakes and stinging scorpions (above), while the Nile had dangerous crocodiles and hippopotamuses. There were also more general threats. If the yearly Nile flood failed, the desert could easily swallow up the fertile land and the crops would fail. The Egyptians performed many rituals to make sure the gods helped their world survive.

A figure of a scarb appears in the cartouche (kahr TOOSH) of Thutmose (thoot MOH suh) III, one of the greatest kings of ancient Egypt. (A cartouche is an oval frame with the name or symbol of a ruler inscribed in it.) Thutmose III ruled from about 1479 to 1425 B.C. Isis wanted to learn Re's (rays) secret name because the Egyptians believed names had a special power. When people died, survivors could help them live on in the afterlife by saying their name out loud. Erasing a dead person's name wherever it appeared was said to destroy the dead person in the afterlife.

RE CREATES
SEKHMET/HATHOR

When Re felt that people had turned against him, he inflicted such terrible punishment on them that he soon began to feel guilty and had to stop people's suffering.

Re (ray), Sun God and Great Father, reigned upon Earth for thousands of years. To him, a century was as a few years. But his human form, like those of his children, slowly began to age. People began to speak contemptuously of the Great Father. "His bones grow weak. His flesh withers," they said.

When Re became aware of this, his heart burned with anger. "Command Shu (shoo), Tefnut (TEHF not), Geb (gehb), and Nut (noot) to come before me!" Re demanded.

All the gods assembled at the sacred city of Heliopolis (hee lee OP uh lihs) in secret, in case people saw them and became terrified that disaster was about to descend on them. Even Nu (noo), God of the First Water, joined the gathering. All the gods bowed to Re and said, "Speak your mind and we will hear."

"Humanity has rebelled against me and has nothing but contempt for me," said Re. "They even seek to slay me, presuming I'm weak. What, O Mighty Ones, is your counsel. How shall it be?"

Nu, Re's father, was first to speak: "Your throne remains secure, Mighty Re. Humankind continues to fear you. Nevertheless, send your All-Seeing Eye against those who rebel against you." The assembled gods agreed with Nu. "Yes, Great Father. Be it so! Send your All-Seeing Eye in the form of Sekhmet (SEHK meht), the Destroyer. Let the rebels perish from your kingdom!"

So Re sent Sekhmet, the Lion Goddess, among the people. The fierce goddess rejoiced in her grim work. She laughed when wading in blood. She grew fat on the flesh of victims. She delighted in the splintering of bone. To her, death screams and tearful cries were sweet music. The more destruction she caused, the greater her blood lust became.

When Re saw that Sekhmet would soon destroy all of humanity, he was sorry for his anger. He sent messengers to the holy city of Elephantine (EHL uh FAN tihn), commanding the people there to quickly gather beneficial herbs and barley. These they mingled and fermented with the blood of the slain. They labored until they had brewed 7,000 jars of this special beer.

Then the people traveled to Dendera (DEHN duh rah), the place where Sekhmet rested each night after her day of slaughter. As Re commanded, they poured out the contents of the jars.

When Sekhmet arose the nexy day, she smiled to see her beautiful face reflected in the pool of beer. She lapped it up eagerly and soon was too drunk to notice the people who were once her prey.

"Return, beautiful goddess," said Re. "Be with me in peace. I will see to it that beautiful maids serve you as priestesses. Your heart will be made glad by sweet offerings of beer at every New Year's festival."

Re's kind words soothed fierce Sekhmet. Her heart became gentle, and she became Hathor (HATH awr), Mother of Milk and Goddess of Joy, Motherhood, and Gratitude. And so it came to pass that when the holy Nile rises and covers Egyptian soil, the faithful pour out beer-offerings to Sekhmet. In remembrance of the anger and mercy of Re, men and women drink beer until, in their drunkenness, the images of Sekhmet and Hathor look the same.

The World of
ANCIENT EGYPT'S GODS

Egyptian gods were worshiped in large temples, such as those at Karnak (KAHR nak) (right) in Luxor, south of Cairo. A complex of four temples, Karnak included a temple to the Sun God Amun-Re (AH muhn ray), which was the largest temple in ancient Egypt. Each temple was either regarded as the home of a certain deity or dedicated to a dead king. The priests' main job was to serve the deity or king, who was represented by a statue in the temple. The king reigning at the time was considered the chief priest of Egypt. Each day, he or other local priests washed and dressed the statue and brought it food. In each city and town, the people worshiped their own special deity as well as the major ones.

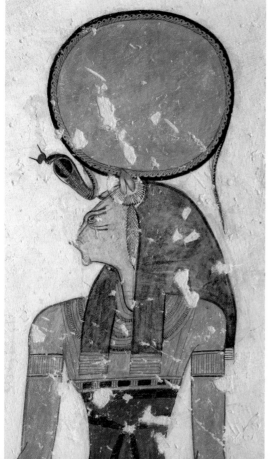

Bastet (BAHS tet), also called Bast (right), was a cat goddess. She was usually represented as a woman with a cat's head. At first, Bastet was almost identical to Sekhmet, a lion goddess of war. But sometime around 1850 B.C., the character of these two goddesses began to differ. Sekhmet became associated more with dangerous and sometimes vicious characteristics. Bastet was seen as more nurturing and protective. In the mid-400's B.C., the Greek historian Herodotus (hih ROD uh tuhs) visited the temple of Bastet in the city of Bubastis (boo bahs tihs), now called Tell Basta. He claimed that 700,000 people made the annual religious journey to the temple. Evidence that Bastet was worshiped widely is seen in the thousands of mummified cats unearthed at archaeological sites throughout Egypt.

LIBATIONS

In the story "Re Creates Sekhmet/Hathor," Re has the people of Dendera (DEHN duh rah) pour a libation to Sekhmet to stop her murderous rampage against humans. A libation is an offering of water or other beverage that is poured on the ground as a sign of reverence and trust. Libations were common in many ancient cultures and are still offered in religious ceremonies today.

Lion-headed Sekhmet (SEHK meht) follows the Sun God Amun-Re in a carving from the Temple to Isis (Y sihs) at Philae (FY lee). Many ancient Egyptian deities were pictured with human bodies and the heads of animals. Such a head suggested a real or imagined quality of the animal and made it easy for ancient Egyptians, who generally could not read or write, to identify the deity.

An obelisk erected by the Pharaoh Senusret (SEH nuhs reht) I in the 1900's B.C. in the ancient city of Heliopolis (hee lee OP uh lihs) symbolized the Sun God Re. Heliopolis, near modern-day Cairo, was a center for the worship of the god. There Re assumed many of the characteristics of Atum (AH tuhm), an early Sun God said to have created the world. By Dynasty V (about 2450–2325 B.C.), Egyptians saw the Sun God as their chief deity. From that time, every Egyptian king was given the title "son of Re."

RE AND THE BOAT OF MILLIONS OF YEARS

Re reigned supreme on Earth, but shortly after he lost his secret name to Isis, he declined again into old age and his heart grew heavy.

"My body lives," said Re (ray), the Sun God, to his children, "but I am world-weary. I no longer desire to dwell on Earth among my human creations. I can no longer go about on my own. I command that you, my divine children, help me."

And so Shu (shoo), the Wind God, and Nut (noot), the Sky Goddess, helped the aging Re. Nut assumed the form of the Heavenly Cow, and Shu lifted Re onto her back. Then Nut carried Re to the heavens. "From now on," Re proclaimed, "my house will be in the heavens. I will no longer reign on Earth."

And it was so. Shining Re made his way through the heavens, putting everything in order. He spoke and Nut gave birth to Aalu (AH loo), the field of stars. The stars gathered at night to praise Re. Re also created the Duat (DOO aht), the underworld, so the spirits of the dead might not rise up to eat the living.

Re spoke to Thoth (thohth), the God of Wisdom: "You take my place on Earth. My messengers—the ibis and the dog-faced ape—now serve you! You must record human deeds so that a fair accounting be made of their lives on the day of Judgment. Deliver the pious, the honest, and the righteous to Amenti (uh MEHN tee), the Land of the Blessed. Bind my enemies in the Duat!"

Having ordered affairs in the heavens, Re set in motion the eternal cycle. Each morning, he burst from Earth as Khephera (keh puhr uh), the scarab beetle. Re-Khephera rolled the sun across the sky as the beetle rolls a ball of dung across the land. At noon, Re was the Radiant One in the fullness of his power. By evening, he was Atum (AH tuhm), the Complete. Re-Atum was an old man who required rest.

During the day, Re sailed Mandjet (mand jeht), his Boat of Millions of Years, across the sky with a company of companions, lighting the world. At night, he sailed the boat Meseket (meh sehk eht) to the underworld, through the Western Gate at the temple of Osiris (oh SY rihs) at Abydos (uh BY duhs). The souls of the newly dead accompanied him. Earth was plunged into darkness for the 12 divisions of night.

Once Re passed through the Western Gates, he sailed upon Urnes, the river of the dead. His companions protected the Sun God with magical spells. During the third division of the night, Meseket docked at the Judgment Hall of Osiris (oh SY rihs). Those who died that day faced Osiris, the Divine Judge. Those who were judged righteous then dwelled with Osiris in Amenti, the Field of Reeds. But the wicked were doomed to the lake of fire where fire-serpents fell upon them with knives, slicing off pieces of their souls.

During the middle of each night, the dragon Apep (AH pehp), God of Shadow, attacked Re. But Re's companions stabbed the serpent with their sacred knives until it retreated. Isis, whose words were power, spoke mighty charms and Re's boat Meseket sailed on unharmed.

At the end of the 12th hour, Re's nighttime journey ended. Riding the Boat of Millions of Years into the eastern sky, the Sun God was reborn, and so the cycle began anew.

The World of
RE THE SUN GOD

Re (ray), also known as Ra (rah), was the Sun God and the most important god in the mythology of ancient Egypt. Usually, he is shown as a man with the head of a falcon, crowned with the disk of the sun and the *uraeus* (yu REE uhs), a cobra symbol. There are more myths and legends about Re than about any other Egyptian god. Some tell about the creation of the world and describe his daily rebirth and perilous journey through the sky and the underworld. Other myths tell about his rule on Earth as king.

The mummy of King Tutankhamun (TOOT ahngk AH muhn) ➥ rests in its original tomb in the Valley of the Kings, near Cairo. Paintings on the walls above the *sarcophagus* (sahr KOF uh guhss) (stone coffin) show the *ka* (soul) of Tutankhamun (white figure, far left) embracing Osiris (oh SY rihs), the chief god of the underworld, on his arrival in the land of the dead. Tutankhamun's father, Akhenaten (AH kuh NAH tehn), had made the Sun God Aten (AH tuhn) the only god of Egypt. But about four years after becoming king, Tutankhamun restored Egypt's old religion.

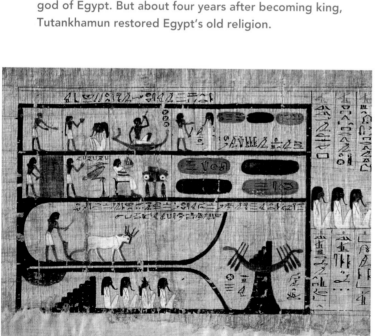

Images and *hieroglyphics* (Egyptian writing symbols) cover a page from the Book of the Dead. The book is actually a collection of texts that was buried with many ancient Egyptians. The texts contain prayers, hymns, spells, and other information to guide souls through the afterlife, protect them from evil, and provide for their needs. Egyptians believed the Book of the Dead helped the spirits of the dead travel through the underworld to Amenti (uh MEHN tee), the Field of Reeds, where they could enjoy a peaceful afterlife. Some copies of the Book of the Dead survive today.

↑

The jackal-headed god Anubis (ah NOO bihs) judges the soul of a dead person at the entrance to the underworld, in a page from a Book of the Dead created in 1250 B.C. for an Egyptian scribe. The ancient Egyptians believed that Anubis used a balance to weigh the dead person's soul against a feather. If the person's soul was lighter than the feather, he or she had lived a pure life and would enjoy paradise in the afterlife.

TRAVELING BY BOAT

Ancient Egyptians believed that the souls of the newly dead traveled to the underworld in Re's boat. For this reason, model boats were often buried with the dead to help them travel through the underworld. Full-sized boats have been found near some pyramids of the Old Kingdom (about 2650 to 2150 B.C.).

The mummy of an ancient Egyptian is transported by boat to a tomb.

The Births of
OSIRIS, ISIS,
NEPTHYS, & SETH

Re, the Sun God, tried to avoid a prophecy that one of his grandchildren would take over his power. Thoth, the god of wisdom, came up with a plan to outwit him.

When Re (ray), the Sun God, still ruled on Earth, he had a dream. He saw that his daughter Nut (noot), the Sky Goddess, would have a son and that this child would replace him on his throne. Re could not bear the thought. He put a curse on Nut that she could not bear children on any day of the year.

Nut was heartbroken. In secret, she consulted with Thoth (thohth), the God of Wisdom. "My heart bursts with longing for children. Yet Re, the Great Father, has forbidden me to bear children on any of the year's 360 days. What can be done, Wise Thoth?"

Thoth thought deeply for some time before saying, "Do not worry, beloved Nut. I know what to do."

Thoth visited Khonsu (KON soo), the Moon God. "Khonsu , my friend, perhaps you'd be interested in a game of senet (sehn iht)?" "What must I wager?" asked Khonsu. "If you lose, you must give me some of your light," replied Thoth.

And so the two gods played, but subtle Thoth won game after game. Khonsu continued to wager some of his light— and continued to lose. Finally he was forced to give up. "You are the better player," sulked Khonsu. "Here is some of my light, for all the good it will do you!" With the light he had won from the Moon God, Thoth fashioned five additional days and added them to the year. Thus the year is now 365 days long. And ever since, the moon does not have sufficient light to shine for a full month. He gives less and less light all month until he must rest to regain his powers.

Because Re's curse affected only the original 360 days of the year, Nut was able to bear children on the new days. On one day, she gave birth to her first son,

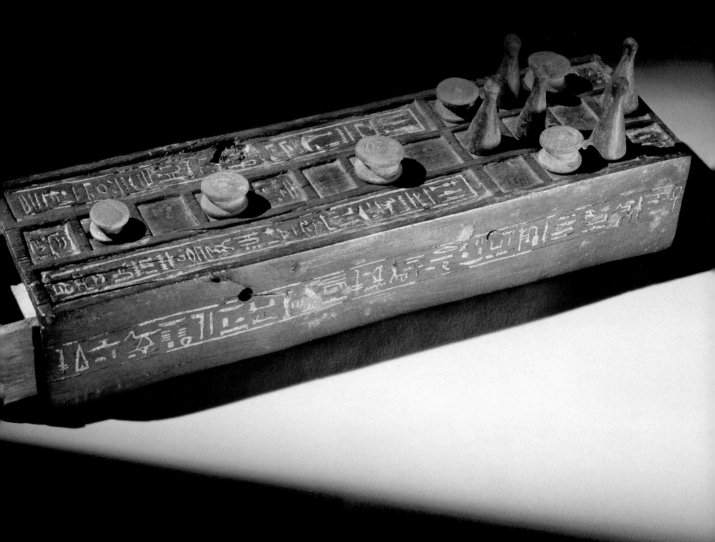

Osiris (oh SY rihs). On another day, she gave birth to the Evil One, Seth (sehth). Then she delivered a daughter, the Radiant Isis (Y sihs). Finally, Isis's sister, the gentle guide Nephthys (NEHF thihs), was born. And so Re's curse was both fulfilled and defeated.

On the day of Osiris's birth, a voice from above proclaimed, "The Lord of All has been born!" The sage Pamyles saw the birth in a vision and was filled with joy. "A good and wise king has been born—Osiris, savior of all!" he exclaimed.

Wise Thoth advised Nut to place the infant Osiris in Pamyles's care. But Thoth instructed both Osiris and Isis in divine wisdom and hidden ways. Isis also convinced Khonsu to teach her the secret ways of the moon, and made herself the most powerful witch ever to have existed.

Gods may only marry other gods, and so, when they came of age, Osiris married Isis and Seth married Nephthys. When Re at last left his mortal form and Osiris assumed his throne, the Egyptians were a rough and ragged lot. They wandered in tribes and hunting bands, fighting with one another.

Seeing that the people were improper and indecent, Osiris established many just laws, served as a wise judge when there were disputes, and taught the people to respect the common good. Eventually, there was an enduring peace in the land and a new age began.

Isis gathered wild grains—barley, wheat, and rye—and gave them to Osiris. He taught the people to plant these seeds and to harvest them in due season. He also taught the people to grind these grains to make meal so there would be food in abundance. As a wise father, Osiris taught his people to train grape vines to grow on poles and to plant fruit trees.

When at last Osiris the Good had secured peace and prosperity for his people, he traveled the world. He wished to show other peoples how to achieve lasting peace and prosperity. Not through battle, but through peaceful persuasion and wisdom did Osiris come to other peoples on Earth. During Osiris's absence, Isis ruled wisely in his place.

The World of OSIRIS

Osiris (oh SY rihs) was one of the most important gods in ancient Egyptian mythology and had many roles. He was often shown as a bearded human mummy with green or black flesh, as in this tomb painting (right). He wears a long white robe and holds a shepherd's crook and *flail* (whip). As a son of the Earth god, Geb (gehb), Osiris was regarded as a source of Earth's *fertility* (productiveness). Ancient Egyptians sometimes compared him to the Nile River. Osiris also became the chief god of the underworld. In Egyptian royal theology, the pharaoh was a living Horus (HAWR uhs), the falcon-headed god who was the son of Osiris. After the pharaoh died, he became Osiris. Egyptian funeral practices later became more democratic, and every Egyptian expected to become an Osiris after death.

Like the gods, the ancient Egyptians loved to play board games. One popular game was senet (sehn iht) (left), which is still played today. It is similar to modern back-gammon. Another popular game was mehen, the snake game. Players moved their counters around a circular board that was shaped like a coiled snake, with its body divided into squares.

EGYPTIAN CALENDAR

The ancient Egyptians were probably the first to adopt a calendar based mainly on the motion of the sun. They noted that the Dog Star, Sirius (SIHR ee uhs), reappeared in the eastern sky just before sunrise after several months of invisibility. They also observed that the annual flood of the Nile River came soon after Sirius reappeared. They used this combination of events to fix their calendar and came to recognize a year of 365 days, made up of 12 months, each 30 days long, and an extra five days added at the end. But they did not allow for the extra fourth of a day, and their calendar drifted into error. According to the famed Egyptologist J. H. Breasted, the earliest recorded date in the Egyptian calendar corresponds to 4236 B.C., in terms of the calendar widely used by western nations.

Ancient Egyptian farmers plant and harvest grain, in a painting from the tomb of an artist. Egyptians believed their ancestors had been taught to farm by Osiris. They grew corn and barley, which they used to make bread and beer. Farmers also grew flax. Its fibers were spun to create a luxury cloth called linen. The best linen was reserved for the pharaoh and the royal family. The cloth was so fine it could be seen through. Other crops included peas and lentils and such fruit as figs.

A farmer uses a hoe to clear the land in a field in the Nile Delta.

SETH AND THE BETRAYAL OF OSIRIS

The ancient Egyptians told the story of Osiris and his betrayal as a reminder that life was a constant struggle between the forces of good and evil. This struggle reflected the constant physical threat to Egypt from the surrounding desert.

The god Seth (sehth), who loved war, envied his brother, the god Osiris (oh SY rihs). As the peace and happiness of the people increased, Seth's hatred for his brother grew stronger. When Osiris hosted a banquet for the gods, Seth brought with him a wooden box so beautifully carved that many people wanted to own it. Seth declared that everyone who wanted the box should lie down inside it, and he would give it to the person whom it fit best.

None suspected treachery. Each person lay down in the box, but the one it fit best was Osiris. Even as the guests cheered the king's good fortune, Seth's followers sprang forward with a lid and nailed it to the box. The box became Osiris's coffin, and the breath left his body. Seth's

henchmen threw Osiris's coffin into the Nile. Hapi (HAH pee), the god of the Nile, carried Osiris's coffin to the sea where it floated for many days.

Eventually, the coffin washed ashore in the country of Phoenicia (fih NIHSH uh) in the shade of a tamarisk tree. The tree soon grew over the casket, spreading forth with many branches and flowers. People came to marvel at the sacred tree, not knowing that within its trunk lay the body of Osiris the Great.

Osiris's body had not been properly prepared, so his spirit remained in the Duat (DOO aht), the underworld. Meanwhile, Seth took Osiris's throne and the land was thrown into disorder. Isis (Y sihs), the wife and sister of Osiris fled

into the marshes of the Nile Delta. Re (ray), the Sun God, was moved to pity by Isis's distress and sent Anubis (uh NOO bihs), the God of Mummification, to guide her to safety. Along the way, Isis gave birth to Horus (HAWR uhs) the Good, but Horus was bitten by a scorpion and died. Immediately, Thoth (thohth), the God of Wisdom, worked a powerful spell. Horus lived again, for it was the will of the gods that he avenge his slain father.

Meanwhile, King Malcander (mal kan duhr) and Queen Astarte (as TAHR tee) of Phoenicia had heard of the wondrous tree. The king ordered the tree cut down and fashioned into a pillar for his palace. Isis learned from a dream that her husband's body was entombed some-

where in Malcander's land. She journeyed to the city of Byblos (BIHB luhs) in disguise, and each day she wept at a well. There she met Queen Astarte's attendants. When they returned to Astarte, the sweet perfume of Isis was upon them. Sensing divine power, the queen commanded the strange woman be brought to her presence.

So Isis became nursemaid to Astarte's son, Dictys (DIHK tees). Each night Isis placed the babe in a sacred flame, for she hoped to give him immortality. One night, however, Astarte disturbed them and, alarmed, snatched her son from the flames, unwittingly breaking Isis's spell.

When Isis confessed her true identity, Astarte offered her any gift her heart desired. Isis asked for the sacred pillar containing Osiris's body, which she loaded aboard her boat. She then set sail for Egypt. Arriving at last at Egypt, Isis hid Osiris's coffin in reeds in the Nile Delta. As fate would have it, Seth was hunting nearby and found the wooden box he'd used to kill his brother. Seth was filled with such hate that he removed Osiris's body and cut it into 14 pieces, which he scattered in the Nile, hoping the crocodiles would eat them.

But the crocodiles feared Isis and refused to eat the pieces of Osiris's body. The god Hapi's great River Nile swept the pieces along, scattering them. When Isis returned to the casket, Osiris's body was gone! She set out to find his remains, and eventually found all but one piece of his body. That piece had been eaten by a fish, which has been considered cursed by Egyptians ever since.

Isis saved the remaining body parts and used her magic to reassemble them and give Osiris a proper burial. Once the body had been properly mourned, prepared, and buried, Osiris's spirit was able to pass to the underworld, where he reigned.

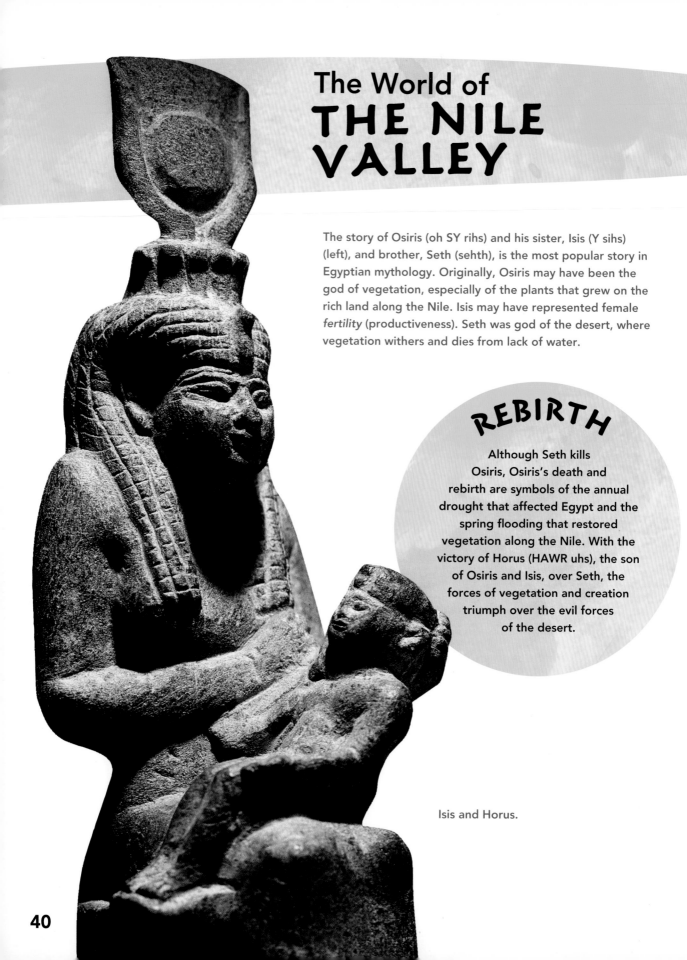

The World of
THE NILE VALLEY

The story of Osiris (oh SY rihs) and his sister, Isis (Y sihs) (left), and brother, Seth (sehth), is the most popular story in Egyptian mythology. Originally, Osiris may have been the god of vegetation, especially of the plants that grew on the rich land along the Nile. Isis may have represented female *fertility* (productiveness). Seth was god of the desert, where vegetation withers and dies from lack of water.

REBIRTH

Although Seth kills Osiris, Osiris's death and rebirth are symbols of the annual drought that affected Egypt and the spring flooding that restored vegetation along the Nile. With the victory of Horus (HAWR uhs), the son of Osiris and Isis, over Seth, the forces of vegetation and creation triumph over the evil forces of the desert.

Isis and Horus.

Beginning in the 1800's, Egyptians replaced the basin irrigation system with a system of year-round irrigation. They built dams, canals, and reservoirs to capture Nile water and make it available throughout the year. The changeover was completed with the building of the Aswan High Dam (below), which began operation in 1968. The dam has increased the amount of land irrigated all year by about 2 million acres (800,000 hectares). However, the dam has resulted in significant environmental problems, including the increased use of polluting fertilizers.

The Nilometer on Elephantine (EHL uh FAN tihn) Island (above) shows the markers used in this device to measure the annual rise and fall of the Nile River. Before modern dams were built on the Nile, the river flooded its valley every summer. Heavy rains in southern Africa drain into the river, causing the water level of the Nile to rise downstream in Egypt. Before dams were built, the Nile would flood its banks by July, covering the land to a distance of about 6 miles (10 kilometers) on either side. Each year, before the flood, farmers created basins on surrounding farmland. When the Nile overflowed, these basins trapped the floodwaters and the *silt* (tiny particles of soil) that they carried. After the floodwaters withdrew in September, farmers planted their fields.

THE BATTLES OF
HORUS AND SETH

For ancient Egyptians, the struggle between Horus and Seth represented the ongoing struggle between good and evil.

The god Seth (sehth) continued his wicked rule over Egypt, persecuting those loyal to the god Osiris (oh SY rihs) and sowing chaos and violence wherever he could. Horus (HAWR uhs), the son of Osiris and Isis (Y sihs), grew into a powerful young man, thirsting to avenge his father's death.

The metal workers in the land fashioned sharp blades and strong spears, knowing war was coming. Meanwhile, the spirit of Osiris visited Horus, teaching him the ways of wisdom and war. "Tell me, my son," said the spirit of Osiris, "what is the greatest duty of all humankind?"

"To avenge the wrongs done to their fathers and mothers," answered Horus. Pleased with this response, Osiris asked, "What animal, then, is best suited to the avenger?" "The horse," replied Horus. "Surely a lion would be the more powerful companion, my son." "Perhaps," the young man said, "but with a horse's

great speed, the avenger can prevent his enemies from escaping."

Considering this, Osiris knew Horus was ready for his destined task. And so Horus declared war on his uncle, Seth. From the Delta lands, Horus's army marched on Seth's army encamped in the southern desert. Bearing red banners emblazoned with the flying hawk, Horus's army advanced and prepared for battle.

Re (ray), the shining father of gods, sailed up the Nile in his Boat of Millions of Years. "Let me look into your eyes," Re said to Horus. "For all gaze into your blue eyes to find the future there. I would see the outcome of this battle."

But wicked Seth saw an opportunity. Transforming himself into a great black boar with fearsome tusks, the Devious One ran into Horus's field of vision, distracting him. "Look!" cried Horus.

"Have you ever seen, Grandfather, a boar so large and fierce as that one?"

Filled with wonder, Horus was caught off guard without a spell to protect him. Seeing him so vulnerable, Seth aimed a fireball at Horus's eyes, destroying one of them. Partially blind and in burning agony, Horus roared in pain and rage. But Seth was gone in an instant, having landed the first blow.

Re took Horus into a dark room and replaced Horus's ruined left eye with the wedjet (wahd geht) eye, which became known as the Eye of Horus. Delighted

that he could again see, Horus resumed the battle. As he and his soldiers sailed up the Nile, spring blossomed.

Horus and Seth fought many battles, but the decisive battle was fought at Edfu (ehd foo), where the great temple of Horus was later built. The armies of these two great enemies fought on the islands surrounded by the dangerous, fast-flowing waters of the Nile, called the First Cataract, not far from Elephantine (EHL uh FAN tihn).

Certain that victory was at hand, Seth transformed himself into a great red

hippopotamus. He uttered a horrible curse, with a voice that rolled like thunder: "Rise up now, O Nile! Descend upon this Upstart and his feeble army, O Storm Winds! Destroy them! Erase their memory from Earth!"

But brave Horus held his course, sailing into the wind and the rising tide. He stood in the prow of his shining boat like a beacon in the gathering darkness. Heaving himself from the waters, Seth opened his hippopotamus jaws, intent on swallowing Horus and his army.

But Horus was ready for him. In his hands was a long harpoon with a wide blade. When Seth opened his jaws, Horus heaved the harpoon into the open jaws, lodging the blade in the brain of his enemy. Seth's enormous hippo form sank beneath the waves, dead. The winds stopped, the storm clouds disappeared, and in their place, the blue sky of a fine day appeared overhead.

Emerging from their homes, the people of Edfu hailed Horus. "Great is Horus, he of the mighty blow! Mighty is the Avenger, wielder of the harpoon! All glory and praise to Horus! Rejoice! Feast on the flesh of the fallen! Drink the blood of the red hippopotamus! Cut him in

pieces and give the scraps to the cats and reptiles of the land!" And so peace and prosperity were restored in Egypt as in the days of Osiris the Good.

But the gods did not dwell forever on Earth. In heaven, Horus and Seth each contended for the rule of Earth. Each made a compelling case. "Many are the pious and good," insisted Horus. "They deserve a good and wise king to ensure their prosperity and secure their peace." "How many more are the violent and wicked?" demanded Seth. "I am their rightful ruler and should oversee their struggles."

Even Thoth (thohth), the God of Wisdom, could not judge between their claims. And so Horus and Seth continued their battle for the souls of men. Sometimes the wicked seemed to prevail. At other times, the righteous gained the upper hand.

And so it is to this day. Some of us Egyptians believe that the Final Battle between Horus and Seth is yet to come. When Seth is at last destroyed, Osiris will return to Earth with the righteous dead. Thus we Egyptians preserve our dead so they may find their bodies intact when they return on that blessed day.

The World of HORUS AND SETH

Early in its history, Egypt was divided into the Upper (southern) and Lower (northern) kingdoms, which were often at war. *Egyptologists*—scholars who study ancient Egypt—today debate which king united Egypt. According to tradition, a king called Menes (MEE neez) ruled Upper Egypt. Many scholars believe Menes may have been the same person as an actual king named Narmer (NAHR muhr). Narmer gained control over Lower Egypt and united the kingdoms in about 3000 B.C. Thereafter, the kings wore the *pschent* (pshehnt), or double crown, shown on the falcon-headed god Horus (HAWR uhs) (far right) in a tomb painting. The crown combined the white crown or tall, pointed miter of southern Egypt with the red crown—square in front and rising to a point behind—of northern Egypt.

When Seth turns into an angry hippopotamus, ancient Egyptians would have known just how dangerous that could be. Although hippos are vegetarians, they are also known to kill people with their huge teeth. The Egyptians worshiped a goddess named Taweret (tah hwair iht), who had the body of a hippo and the head of a crocodile (left). These were both animals the Egyptians respected but also feared. Taweret was the protector of mothers and children, but she could also be a ferocious demon.

The Nile River is the longest river in the world. It flows generally northward for 4,160 miles (6,695 kilometers) through northeast Africa. For this reason, the southernmost part of the river is called the Upper Nile and the northernmost part is called the Lower Nile.

The Nile rises near the equator and flows into the Mediterranean Sea. It irrigates about 6 million acres (2.4 million hectares) of land in Egypt and about 2 ¾ million acres (1.1 million hectares) in Sudan. For much of Egypt and Sudan, the Nile is the sole source of water.

THE CATARACTS

For most of its way north, the Nile flows smoothly and slowly. But in several places, it passes over stretches of rock. Here the water is much shallower, and it runs quickly around many boulders and small islands. These stretches of rocky rapids are called *cataracts* (KAT uh rakts). There are six main Nile cataracts. The first (farthest north) is at Aswan (AS wahn) in present-day Egypt. In ancient times, this was as far as boats could travel upstream, unless they were *portaged* (carried overland) or passed through canals dug to bypass the cataract.

A fisher casts his net into the Nile. Fish from the river have long been an important source of food for the Egyptians.

47

THUTMOSE
AND THE SPHINX

The ancient Egyptians told this story to praise King Thutmose IV and to explain the origins of the Sphinx, one of Egypt's most famous monuments.

King Amenhotep (uh mehn HOH tehp) had many sons, but Thutmose (thoot MOH suh) was his favorite. The king was not alone in his admiration for the lad. People often remarked that in courage and fighting skill, Thutmose was like Horus (HAWR uhs) the Brave, who defeated his father's enemies. Even so, Thutmose was far down the line to inherit his father's throne. In addition to Horus, Thutmose was outranked by several other older brothers.

Thutmose's brothers were envious of their younger brother. They feared that their father would do away with them so that Thutmose could inherit the throne.

Such discontent upset Thutmose, so he went to the temple of Re (ray), the Sun God, to pray for peace with his brothers.

Thutmose loved hunting and riding chariots above all other sports. Early one morning, Thutmose and his friends mounted their chariots and raced into the desert to hunt lions and gazelles. Careening over the dunes, Thutmose and his companions brought their steeds up short when they came to an enormous head poking out of the sand.

They had been riding all day, so they rode closer to the wonder and rested in its shade. Soon, Thutmose fell into a

deep sleep and began to dream. Re-Harmakhis (ray HAHRM mah kahs), also known as the Sphinx (sfihngks), appeared in his dream and spoke to him.

"I am your father, Thutmose," said the mighty Re-Harmakhis. "My heart has turned toward you to make you great. I will place both the White and Red crowns upon your head. The Upper and Lower kingdoms will be united under your rule. All of Egypt's wealth will be yours, and kings and princes from far lands will bring you tribute. Behold how the sands have almost buried my image! All that

I have shown you will be yours if you remove the sands burying my image. Show my Sphinx form to the world and all will know you are my favored son."

Thutmose organized workers to remove the sands covering the Sphinx. As promised, the young prince's fame grew, and he soon became king.

The World of THE SPHINX

The Great Sphinx (sfihngks) at Giza (GEE zuh), built some 4,500 years ago, has the head of a human and the body of a reclining lion. The world's largest and oldest monumental sculpture, it measures 240 feet (73 meters) long and rises about 66 feet (20 meters) high. Historians don't know what the creators of the Sphinx called their statue, but by the time of Thutmose (thoot MOH suh) IV, it was called *Horus (HAWR uhs) of the Horizon.*

The story of Thutmose and the Sphinx comes from an ancient object called the Dream Stele (STEE lee). A stele is an upright pillar or slab of stone into which writing or a design has been carved. The stele was erected by Pharaoh Thutmose IV, who ruled from about 1400 to 1390 B.C. Some experts think that Thutmose was not supposed to become pharaoh, because he was not the previous king's oldest son. But Thutmose pushed his older brother aside and seized the throne. He may have made up the story of his dream about the Sphinx to show his subjects that the gods had made him the rightful ruler.

The head and body of the Great Sphinx was carved directly out of a giant rock in a limestone formation. Stone blocks cut from the formation were used to form the paws and legs. The Great Sphinx wears a royal headdress and lies near the pyramid of King Khafre (KAF ray), who ruled from about 2520 to 2494 B.C. Historians believe that the Sphinx's face may be a portrait of Khafre, who probably had the monument built. Sand has often buried the Great Sphinx up to its neck. During modern times, workers removed the sand in 1818, 1886, 1926, and 1938.

Thutmose offers incense to the god Re-Harmakhis (ray HAHRM mah kahs) in the form of a sphinx, in a detail of the Dream Stele.

SPHINX

The ancient Egyptians were not the only peoples who told stories about sphinxes or created images of them. Other peoples of the Near East also had stories about sphinxes. According to various tales, the sphinx had the body of a lion and the head of a human, falcon, or ram. Some sphinxes also had wings and a serpent tail. The term *sphinx* is a Greek word that originally referred to an legendary monster. The ancient Greeks used the term to describe the stone statues of lions with human heads that they saw during visits to Egypt.

Most Egyptian sphinxes had the head of a human and the body, feet, and tail of a lion. Others had heads of rams or falcons. Egyptians often carved sphinxes to honor a king or queen. The sculptors modeled the face of such a sphinx after the honored person. Egyptian art often showed kings as lions conquering their enemies, and sphinxes became symbols of royal protection. Statues of sphinxes lined avenues leading to temples, such as those near the great temple at Karnak (KAHR nak). Other sphinxes represented the god Horus (HAWR uhs), who was thought to be a protector of the king.

SE-OSIRIS AND SETNA

VISIT THE UNDERWORLD

For the ancient Egyptians, this story illustrated why it was more important to live a just and true life than it was to be rich.

One day Setna (SEHT nuh), the scribe, and his young son, Se-Osiris (seh oh SY rihs), watched two funeral processions. The first procession was for a rich man. His coffin was followed by a large crowd. The second procession was for a poor worker. His coffin was a cheap wooden box, and his only mourners were his wife and his two sons.

"Hmm," murmured Setna, "I hope my funeral is more like that of the rich man." "Oh, no!" exclaimed Se-Osiris, "I hope that you share the worker's fate. Come, I will show you! Each *ba* (bah), the part of our soul that makes us unique, will travel to the Duat (DOO aht) where the dead go to be judged and see all that happens there. There you will see how very different are the fates of these two dead men."

So Setna and his son made their way to the temple of the god Osiris, where Se-Osiris drew a magic circle upon the floor, lit a small fire, and uttered a word of power. The entire temple shuddered and all went dark within. Setna understood that his ba had left his body and was now able to move on its own. "Follow me, Father," said the disembodied voice of Se-Osiris. "We have only until morning to return." Turning toward the voice, Setna saw the body of a great bird with the face of his son. So this was what the ba within looked like!

Swift as arrows they shot westward. Soon they beheld below them the Sun God Re's (rays) boat departing with Re for his nightly trip through the underworld. The gates of the Duat opened to permit Re's boat, laden with the kas (kahs), the life powers, of all those who had died that day, to enter Osiris's Judgment Hall.

Setna and Se-Osiris went with them. The newly dead left Re's boat. Osiris met them, wrapped in his mummy's bandages. On his head was the uraeus (yu REE uhs), the Cobra Crown. His arms were crossed over his chest, and he clutched a flail in one hand and a

shepherd's crook in another. Anubis (uh NOO bihs), the jackal-headed god, stood next to a set of weighing scales.

Each *ka* uttered the same cry, "I am pure! I come to you without sin, without guilt or evil! I have made the offerings required and satisfied the gods' demands! Protect me from Apep (AH pehp), Eater-of-Souls! Protect me, Lord of Breath, Osiris the Great."

Then into the scales the heart of each ka was placed and balanced against the Feather of Truth. The hearts of those heavy with evil sank so low that Ammit

(AH miht), the Devourer of Hearts, reached up and swallowed them. The evil-doers were banished to the Fiery Pit, there to be tormented by Apep the Terrible. This was the fate of the ka of the rich man whose lavish funeral procession Setna and his son had witnessed.

The heart of the good, however, rose higher and higher, as the Feather of Truth tipped the scales in the opposite direction. Horus (HAWR uhs) led the good by their hands before Osiris's throne and pronounced them pure. They passed in joy to Amenti (uh MEHN tee), the Field of Reeds, where they dwelled in happiness. Among these *kas* was that of the poor man with the small funeral procession.

Se-Osiris spoke at last to his father, "Do you now see why I wished for you the fate of the poor man? For the rich man now suffers eternal torment. However, the poor laborer lives in the land of the Blessed."

With that, the *bas* of the father and the son took wing and returned to their bodies lying in Osiris's temple. Just as the sun began to rise, they rose up, ready to return to their ordinary lives.

The World of THE SCRIBE

Scribes were among the most important people in ancient Egypt because relatively few Egyptians could read and write. The scribes were responsible for keeping records of the royal family and the great temples as well as important events and the calculations of taxes. They also read and wrote letters for Egyptians who could not read and write. It is partly because of the scribes' records that we know so much about ancient Egypt today.

Scribes had special tools for smoothing papyrus (puh PY ruhs) and mixing ink.

The king's palace, government departments, and temples operated schools for scribes. Only a small percentage of children went to these schools, and most of them came from upper-class families. Some girls were trained as scribes, though this was not common. Scribes trained for many years to be able to write using *hieroglyphics* (picture symbols) as well as quicker types of writing known as hieratic and demotic. Egyptian scribes wrote on clay tablets or on papyrus, the world's first paperlike material.

Papyrus is a reedy marsh grass that grows abundantly in the Nile River Valley.

⬅ The ancient Egyptians used papyrus to make many items, including boats, sandals, mats, baskets, and ropes. Most famously, they used papyrus to make a form of paper. The word *paper* comes from *papyrus*. The Egyptians made papyrus by laying strips of mashed fiber from the plant's stem in layers. Then they applied pressure to the layers. The crushed strips matted into a loose-textured, porous, white paper. Papyrus was first used as a writing material in Egypt more than 4,700 years ago.

THE HUMAN SOUL

The ancient Egyptians believed the human soul was composed of five parts: the *ka* (kah), the *ba* (bah), the *ren* (rehn), the *sheut*, and the *ib* (ihb). The ka, the "life force," was the power giving energy to the body. The body dies when the ka leaves. The ba, a person or thing's personality or nature, was believed to survive death and live forever in the afterlife. The ren, the name a person was given at birth, was believed to have magical power that survived so long as it was written down or remembered by another. The sheut was one's shadow. Because the shadow always accompanies the body, the Egyptians believed it was part of the person. The ib, the heart, was believed to be the seat of emotion, thought, and will.

Hieroglyphics cover the sides of an ancient Egyptian obelisk (OB uh lihsk) that now stands in Paris.

DEITIES OF ANCIENT EGYPT

Amun (AH muhn)

One of the "Great Ennead" (the nine original beings who existed before Earth and humans), Amun was the creator of the universe and the Egyptian Sky God. He ended his rivalry with Re by joining with him and becoming "Amun-Re."

Anubis (uh NOO bihs)

Anubis, the jackal-headed God of the Underworld, was the patron of embalming. He held the scales to measure the weight of the hearts of the newly dead which decided whether they went on to heaven or hell.

Atum (AH tuhm)

Known as the One Who Completes, Atum was a Sun God in early Egyptian mythology and the creator of heaven and Earth. He was also the father of Shu and Tefnut. Human beings sprang from his tears.

Bastet (BAHS tet)

Re's daughter Bastet was originally a lion-headed goddess but changed into the popular cat-headed goddess. Cats were sacred in ancient Egypt, and a yearly festival was held in Bastet's honor. First associated with the sun, Bastet became associated with fertility, love, and motherhood as her worship spread to other places in Egypt.

Geb (gehb)

The Earth Father, Geb was the twin brother of Nut. He was also known as Seb.

Great Ennead (EHN ee ad)

The Great Ennead was a family of nine gods. Their name comes from the Greek word *ennea,* meaning *nine.* The gods of the Great Ennead were Atum, Shu, Tefnu, Geb, Nut, Osiris, Isis, Nephthys, and Horus. The term *Ennead* later came to include other deities as well.

Hapi (HAH pee)

The God of the Nile, Hapi was most often shown holding ears of corn and *cornucopia* (horns of plenty), the offerings he received from Egyptians hoping to secure the yearly Nile flooding that fertilized the farming land.

Hathor (HATH awr)

The Goddess of Love and Happiness, Hathor was shown as a cow and was often invoked as a protector of women.

Horus (HAWR uhs)

Falcon-headed Horus the Good, the son of Osiris and Isis, lost an eye fighting the god Seth to avenge his father's death. One eye was the sun, and the one he lost was the moon, which is now worn by Osiris in the Underworld.

Isis (Y sihs)

Mother-goddess of Egypt, Isis had to go to the ends of Earth to find the body of her murdered husband, Osiris.

Khephera (keh puhr uh)

A scarab beetle who every morning pushed his dung-ball up the hill to represent the Sun God Re's pushing the sun across the sky. Khephera was the god of rebirth.

Khonsu (KON soo)

Khonsu was a Moon God. Unusually for moon gods, he was a young man and enjoyed intellectual puzzles and solving riddles.

Nephthys (NEHF thihs)

A funerary goddess, Nepthys provided comfort and moral support to people mourning a death.

Nu (noo)

Another member of the "Great Ennead," Nu was the Egyptian Water God and had a frog's head. He sailed around the world on a boat powered by the sun's rays.

Nut (noot)

The Creation Goddess Nut was also the Egyptian Sky Goddess who held the heavens in the hollow of her back. She was always depicted as a giant blue woman, covered in stars.

Osiris (oh SY rihs)

Osiris used to be the god of vegetation and fertility before a battle with his brother Seth, who chopped his body into many pieces. Luckily for Osiris, his wife Isis gathered the pieces together and saved him from death. He became the hugely important Judge of the Dead in the underworld.

Re (ray)

Re, the All-Seeing Eye, was by far the most important Egyptian god. Human beings were made from his tears. As the God of the Sun, he was originally Atum, the One Who Completes. He created Shu and Tefnut to make the world.

Sekhmet (SEHK meht)

The lion-headed Sekhmet, who became Hathor, was a quick-tempered goddess and once destroyed humans. Also known as the Eye of the Sun, Sekhmet was a goddess of healing.

Seth (sehth)

Seth was a violent and destructive god, in charge of causing chaos. After he murdered his brother, Osiris, he was banished to the far reaches of heaven and became the sound of the thunder.

Shu (shoo)

The Wind God Shu noticed one day that Earth and sky were not staying properly apart. So he stood between the two to keep them at a safe distance.

Tefnut (TEHF not)

Lion-headed (like Sekhmet), Tefnut, Giver of Rain, was the bringer of rain, goddess of water, and twin sister of Shu. She made the dew form.

Thoth (thohth)

Ibis-headed Thoth, the Egyptian God of Wisdom, was responsible for the hieroglyphs and the development of the law, among many other achievements.

GLOSSARY

Afterlife Existence after death.

Book of the Dead A collection of religious or magical texts that was buried with a dead body in a tomb.

creation The process by which the universe was brought into being at the start of time.

delta A fan-shaped region of streams and islands at the mouth of a river.

dynasty A succession of rulers who all share the same origins or come from the same family. Egyptian history is divided into more than 30 dynasties.

embalmed Describes a body that has been specially treated to prevent it decaying after death.

flax A blue-flowered plant whose fibers are used to make a fine textile called linen.

hieratic An ancient Egyptian writing system that was quicker to use than hieroglyphics.

hieroglyphics A writing system that uses small pictures to stand for sounds or ideas.

ibis A large wading bird with a curved beak.

irrigation A system of basins and canals used to artificially water fields.

myth A traditional story that a people tell to explain their own origins or the origins of natural and social phenomena. Myths often involve gods, spirits, and other supernatural beings.

papyrus A material made from the fibrous stems of the papyrus plant, which the ancient Egyptians used for writing on.

pharaoh The title used for the king later in ancient Egyptian history.

pschent The "double crown" of Egypt, which combined the red crown of Lower Egypt and the white crown of Upper Egypt.

pyramids Large structures with a square base that either taper toward a point at the top or rise in a series of steps, each smaller than the one below.

ritual A solemn religious ceremony in which a set of actions are performed in a specific order.

sacred Something that is connected with the gods or goddesses and so should be treated with respectful worship.

sacrifice An offering made to a god or gods, often in the form of an animal or even a person who is killed for the purpose. Sacrifices also take the shape of valued possessions that might be buried, placed in caves, or thrown into a lake for the gods.

sanctuary A part of a temple that is considered particularly holy.

scribe A person who copies out documents, keeps records, and reads and writes for those people who cannot read or write.

scrolls Long, thin documents that are stored by being rolled up.

shrine A holy place associated with a particular deity.

sphinx A mythological creature with a lion's body and the head of a human or another type of animal.

supernatural Describes something that cannot be explained by science or by the laws of nature, which is therefore said to be caused by such beings as gods, spirits, or ghosts.

FOR FURTHER INFORMATION

Books

Bell, Michael, and Sarah Quie. *Ancient Egyptian Civilization* (Ancient Civilizations and Their Myths and Legends). Rosen Central, 2010.

Doyle, Sheri. *Understanding Egyptian Myths* (Understanding Myths). Crabtree Publishing Company, 2012.

Fleming, Fergus, and Alan Lothian. *Ancient Egypt's Myths and Beliefs.* (World Mythologies). Rosen Publishing Group, 2012.

Fletcher, Joann. *Exploring the Life, Myth, and Art of Ancient Egypt* (Civilizations of the World). Rosen Publishing Group, 2010.

Green, Roger Lancelyn, and Heather Copley. *Tales of Ancient Egypt* (Puffin Classics). Puffin, 2011.

Hart, George. *Ancient Egypt* (DK Eyewitness Books). DK Publishing, 2014.

Hibbert, Clare. *Terrible Tales of Ancient Egypt* (Monstrous Myths). Gareth Stevens Publishing, 2014.

Limke, Jeff. *Isis and Osiris: To the Ends of the Earth* (Graphic Myths and Legends). Graphic Universe, 2007.

Macdonald, Fiona. *Egyptian Myths and Legends* (All About Myths). Capstone Raintree, 2013.

Napoli, Donna Jo. *Treasury of Egyptian Mythology: Classic Stories of Gods, Goddesses, Monsters, and Mortals* (National Geographic Kids). National Geographic Society, 2013.

National Geographic Essential Visual History of World Mythology. National Geographic Society, 2008.

Orr, Tamra. *Ancient Egypt* (Explore Ancient Worlds). Mitchell Lane Publishers, 2013.

Philip, Neil. *Eyewitness Mythology* (DK Eyewitness Books). DK Publishing, 2011.

Remler, Pat. *Egyptian Mythology A to Z, (Mythology A to Z)*. Chelsea House Publishers, 2010.

Schomp, Virginia. *The Ancient Egyptians* (Myths of the World). Marshall Cavendish Benchmark, 2008.

Websites

http://www.godchecker.com/pantheon/egyptian-mythology.php
A directory of Egyptian deities from God Checker, written in a light-hearted style but with accurate information.

http://www.pantheon.org/areas/mythology/africa/egyptian/
Encyclopedia Mythica page with links to many pages about Egyptian myths. Click on the link to "available articles."

http://www.mythome.org/egypturl.html
A page with links to articles and pages about all aspects of Egyptian life and mythology.

http://www.crystalinks.com/egypt.html
This Crystal Links page has links to pages about all aspects of ancient Egypt, including its gods, goddesses, and myths.

http://www.bbc.co.uk/history/ancient/egyptians/
A BBC website that includes articles on ancient Egyptian history and culture, images of Egyptian artifacts, and interactive games.

INDEX

PRONUNCIATION KEY	
Sound	**As in**
a	hat, map
ah	father, far
ai	care, air
aw	order
aw	all
ay	age, face
ch	child, much
ee	equal, see
ee	machine, city
eh	let, best
ih	it, pin, hymn
k	coat, look
o	hot, rock
oh	open, go
oh	grow, tableau
oo	rule, move, food
ow	house, out
oy	oil, voice
s	say, nice
sh	she, abolition
u	full, put
u	wood
uh	cup, butter
uh	flood
uh	about, ameba
uh	taken, purple
uh	pencil
uh	lemon
uh	circus
uh	labyrinth
uh	curtain
uh	Egyptian
uh	section
uh	fabulous
ur	term, learn, sir, work
y	icon, ice, five
yoo	music
zh	pleasure